Sea Urchins and SAND PIGS

Cornelia Funke

With illustrations by
Sarah Horne

Barrington Stoke

N

Rocks

Pebbly Bay

Mermaid Rock

Rocks

Cliff Edge

Rock Pool

Tom's Cottage

Ella's Cottage

Anna + Max's Cottage

Ben's Cottage

Mia's Cottage

Joe + Grandpa's Cottage

SHOP

The Park

CAFE

Sandy Beach Cove

For Lucan

First published in Great Britain in 2014 by
Barrington Stoke Ltd
18 Walker Street, Edinburgh, EH3 7LP

www.barringtonstoke.co.uk

Title of the original German edition:
Leselöwen – Strandgeschichten
© 2007 Loewe Verlag GmbH, Bindlach

Illustrations © 2014 Sarah Horne
Translation © 2014 Barrington Stoke

The moral right of Cornelia Funke and Sarah Horne to be
identified as the author and illustrator of this work has been
asserted in accordance with the Copyright, Designs and
Patents Act, 1988

A CIP catalogue record for this book is available
from the British Library upon request

ISBN: 978-1-78112-390-4

Printed in China by Leo

This book has dyslexia friendly features

Contents

1   Mia and the Message in a Bottle   1

2   Joe and the Sand Pigs   21

3   Anna and the Little Boy Lost   47

4   Tom and Nipper   65

5   Ben and the Shell Surprise   85

Mia and the Message in a Bottle

The tenth day of the holidays started off the same as all the others.

After breakfast, Mia's family drove down to the beach. Dad found a shady place to read his paper. Mum and Mia's big sister Nora rubbed on sun cream until their skin was all shiny, and then they lay down in the sun.

Mia found this boring, so she started to play "Salt and Pepper". In this game, Mia sprinkled sand on Nora's sticky belly till Nora got mad and chased her around the beach.

It was good fun. But Nora wasn't in the mood today. She just wiped the sand off. "Buzz off, squirt," she said. "Go and build a sandcastle or something."

Mia didn't want to build a silly, babyish sandcastle and there was no space for a proper big sandcastle in between all the sunbathers. So Mia sat down, dug her toes into the sand and stared out to sea.

Dad had promised that he would take her for an ice cream at 1 p.m. It was a long time until then.

The sea licked Mia's toes. An empty sun-cream tub floated past in the sea, and then a lolly stick, a sandal and a green bottle. Mia could see something in the bottle. It looked like a rolled up piece of paper ...

It was a message in a bottle!

Mia looked around. No one else seemed to have spotted the bottle. Mia ran into the water and fished it out. Then she sat down again in the sand and peeked through the glass. Yes, there was a rolled up piece of paper in there, and there was something written on it.

Mia tried to pull the cork out with her fingers. Then she tried with her teeth. At last, it came out.

The paper was a bit wet. Mia
unrolled it with her sandy fingers.
It said –

**Solve this clue to win the
treasure. Follow the five
black stones to the blue dots.**

Mia looked around. Black stones? How was she supposed to find black stones on a busy beach?

Mia got up and strolled along the water's edge. And, sure enough, there was a black stone!

A little bit further along, Mia found a second stone. A lady was just about to put her beach bag on it.

The third stone was on a towel and the fourth one was on top of a sandcastle.

Mia picked it up and looked around again.

Where was the fifth stone?

Mia could see lots of faces she didn't know. She could see beach umbrellas, bare bellies, tatty newspapers, half-eaten sandwiches, but ...

There it was! Black and smooth. Mia picked the stone up. Now she had to find something with blue dots on.

"Maybe it's a ball," Mia muttered. "Or a towel."

Someone giggled behind her. Mia turned around. She saw a girl about her own age, grinning at her.

"Hello," the girl said. "I'm Ella." Her swimsuit had at least a hundred blue dots on it.

"I claim my treasure," Mia said. "I found you!"

Ella's grin grew even bigger. She handed Mia a crab claw.

"That's the best thing I've found on the beach so far," she said. "I've found a few things. But most of the time I'm a bit bored. How about you?"

Mia nodded as she opened and closed the crab claw. "Where are your parents?" she asked.

Ella pointed to two deckchairs. "Asleep. So I need to make my own fun."

For the rest of the holiday, Mia and Ella spent every moment together. They were always on the look-out for treasure, but they never found anything as good as the crab claw again. They sent more messages in bottles.

Ella wrote the messages. Mia threw the bottles into the water. Then they painted stones black, made little paths, and watched who took their messages out of the sea.

Joe and the Sand Pigs

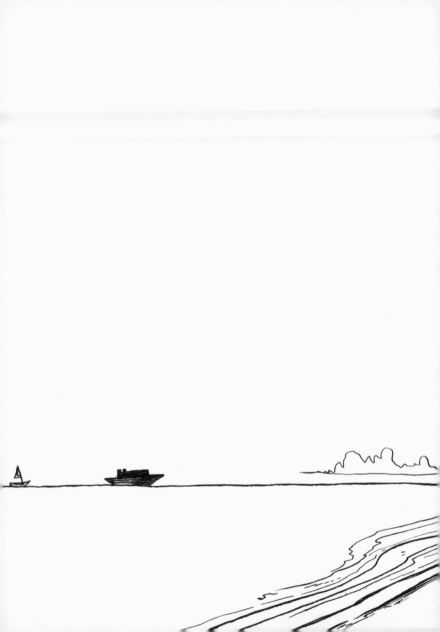

Joe didn't like the sea. He wasn't a good swimmer, and sometimes it felt like the sea was a big wet animal about to swallow him.

But Joe loved the beach. Where else could you build massive sandcastles with towers and moats, sea-shell roofs and long tunnels which felt lovely and cool when you put your sunburned arms in?

Joe loved digging. At home, the children next door teased him because he still had a sandpit, but he didn't mind.

Joe and his grandpa had a cottage very near the beach, and so they always got there early. Joe would search for a place close to the water and get his tools ready – bucket, spade, watering can, and a few sticks of different sizes.

As the beach filled up, Grandpa would vanish behind a newspaper in his deckchair and Joe would set to work.

One morning, Joe made a hill that was nearly a metre high. The moat around the hill was so big that Joe could kneel in it. He flattened the top of the hill and built walls, stairs, gates and towers for his castle.

Last of all, Joe started to dig a tunnel into the hill. That was always the best bit. Joe imagined the vaults at the end of the tunnel – secret treasure chambers and dungeons where the lord of the castle would throw his enemies. Joe's fingers kept digging. His arm was deep under the castle when his fingers touched something soft.

Joe pulled his arm back so fast that he tore a big hole in the castle hill. He patted the sand down again. Then, with great care, he put his arm back into the tunnel.

There! It was there again.
Something warm and downy. Joe tried
to grab it, but claws scratched him. He
pulled his arm out and looked into the
dark hole.

There were two eyes glowing in the dark. They were narrow and green. Then a small, pink face shot out of the hole and looked around. "Do you have any sun cream?" it whispered.

Joe was lost for words. He found his sun cream and held it up.

"We don't like that kind," the little face whispered, and it vanished back into the sand.

Joe stared at the castle. He was struck dumb, as if the little furry something had hit him over the head with a spade.

"Hey," he whispered into the tunnel.
"Are you a sand ... mole or something?"

He heard whispering in the dark.
And then the little furry face appeared
again. "Sand pigs! We are sand pigs," it
muttered. "Have you got any crisps?"

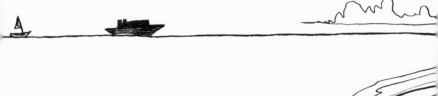

Joe shook his head. "Sorry, no," he said.

The sand pig turned up its nose and vanished.

"Hey, wait!" Joe shouted into the tunnel. "I could build a hide-out for you."

Joe didn't wait for an answer. He rushed to build a high wall of sand and stones around the castle moat.

That didn't hide the castle as much as he had hoped. So then Joe planted some sticks between the towers and hung his towel over them, so that the castle and its tunnel were hidden behind a canopy.

Then he put his head and shoulders
under the towel and whispered into the
tunnel. "You can come up now, little
sand pigs. Please! Nobody can see you.
I promise!"

For a while nothing moved. But then
three little furry creatures sniffled and
snuffled their way out of the tunnel.

The sand pigs climbed up the castle hill, then jumped over the walls and started to explore. They ran up the stairs and climbed the towers, as if they had always lived there.

One of the towers collapsed and a little sand pig rolled down the castle hill, but Joe managed to catch it before it rolled out from behind the towel.

Joe patted the sand off the pig and put it back inside the castle walls. He was just about to make the sand pig a little seat, when the towel lifted and Grandpa appeared.

As quick as a flash, the sand pigs scrambled back into the tunnel.

"Shall we go for an ice cream?"
Grandpa said.

"No, thank you. I'd rather keep
digging," Joe said. "But can you get me
some crisps, please?"

"No ice cream?" Grandpa shook his
head in surprise. As he walked off, Joe
vanished behind the towel again.

"You'll get your crisps in a minute!"
he whispered. "Just stay in the tunnel
till I call you!"

Joe had just finished making three
sand chairs and a table when Grandpa
lifted the towel again. "It's not bad, your
castle," he said, and he dropped a bag of
crisps in the empty moat.

"Thanks, Grandpa," Joe said. "See you later!" And he tugged the towel down again.

He looked down to see that one of the sand pigs had poked its nose out of the tunnel – and now it was sniffing about.

"I heard rustling!" it said. "I'm sure I did!"

Joe smiled and put a handful of crisps on the table. In a flash, the three sand pigs ran over and tucked in.

"Wow, I wish you lived with me," Joe said.

"Is there any sand where you live?" the fattest sand pig said, as he chomped away at his crisps.

"Of course!" Joe said. "And I would always have a supply of crisps for you."

The sand pigs started to whisper to one another.

Two weeks later, Joe and his grandpa went home. Joe's backpack was a bit heavier than it had been when they arrived. After all, there were three little sand pigs inside.

Anna and the Little Boy Lost

Little brothers are wonderful when you snuggle up to them in bed, or tickle their fat little feet, or laugh when they get words in a muddle.

But looking after little brothers is hard work. Even harder when you are on the beach and it is teeming with people and you would much rather build a sandcastle than spend all your time fishing your little brother out of the sea.

Anna's little brother Max was quite scared of the sea. But that didn't stop him running in too far. When the sea was calm and still, Max would sing at the top of his voice. But when the waves hit his belly, he would shout at them and try to hit them. He would even race them.

"I'm the winner!" he would say when he sat down again in the warm sand, all tired out. "I won, stupid sea."

That was a bit silly. But it was very funny for Anna, who was 8 and a good swimmer.

"I can swim too," Max said, when Anna took his hand to go for a paddle in the sea. Anna wasn't allowed to point out that he couldn't! If she did, Max would let go of her hand and stomp ahead alone, and Anna would worry that he'd fall over and disappear under the water.

That happened at least once a day.
Even when Anna ran to pick him up, Max
screamed like a hundred little devils.
And then their mum would leap up from
her towel and shout at Anna. "Anna,
please keep an eye on your brother!"

How was Anna supposed to do that
with a brother who got so very angry
and who thought he was stronger and
faster than the whole vast sea?

One day in the middle of their holiday, Anna and Max were building the best sandcastle ever while their mum sunbathed on her towel.

Anna decided that they needed a flagpole for the very top of the castle. "I'm going to look for a lolly stick," she told Max. "You stay here and look after the castle. And make sure you don't wander off."

There were always lots of lolly sticks on the beach. But today Anna just could not find any.

She looked and looked – and perhaps she looked for a little too long ...

By the time Anna got back to the sandcastle, Max was gone.

Anna got such a fright that she
couldn't breathe. At first, she wanted
to wake her mum. But then she noticed
a trail of little footprints. They did not
lead to the water. They led to the café.

Anna began to run.

"Max!" she shouted. "Silly sausage!
Where are you?"

But all Anna could see were beach umbrellas and grown-ups sleeping under them.

'How am I supposed to find Max when he is so small?' she thought.

Her hands felt empty without her brother's fat little fingers in her own. She wanted to find him so much that she would have let him throw sand in her hair or steal her chocolate.

"Maaaax!" Anna shouted. Everyone stared at her – but then she spotted him! He was in front of the café, small and lost, rubbing his wet eyes.

Anna ran. She jumped over legs, beach bags and empty towels. She stubbed her toe on a windbreak ... And then she got Max in such a tight hug that she squeezed all the air out of him.

Max rubbed his snotty nose on Anna's arm. "Lady not let me buy ice cream!" he sobbed. He showed Anna a penny in his fat little hand. It was nowhere near enough for an ice cream.

"Max!" Anna said in a very strict voice. "You can't just wander off like that. What if you fell in a rock pool or some pirates kidnapped you?"

Max sniffed. "But I am big boy now," he said, and he wiped his nose on her arm again.

"Oh, Max," Anna said and gave him another big hug. "Let's go back to Mum and you can ask her to buy us an ice cream, OK?"

"You can ask if you like," Max said.

But Anna said, "No, no, no. I think I'll let you do that."

Because Anna knew that one of the best things about little brothers was that parents found it very hard to say "no" to them.

Tom and Nipper

Tom's grandmother lived in an old house by the sea. There were no cafés or beach huts, just a small path which started behind the house and wound across boggy grasslands to a pebbly bay.

68

Tom had never met anyone else in
that bay. The sharp, grey-green grass
grew almost to the edge of the water.
There were rocks for Tom to climb
on, and sometimes he saw wild swans
swimming out to sea. He collected sea
shells, threw pebbles into the waves and
watched the cows graze on the other
side of the bay.

Tom's parents preferred the beach at Sandy Cove, where they could swim in the warm sea, and eat ice creams at the café. But Tom missed the pebbly bay, where he had the sea all to himself. So he was very happy when the holiday village put up a poster to ask children to help clear the rubbish from a pebbly bay near by.

It only took half an hour for Tom to fill his bag with rubbish that had been washed up by the sea into the lonely bay. "Where does it all come from – the empty bottles, old shoes, tins and plastic bags?" he asked himself. From the other side of the world, or some ship far out at sea?

Behind a rock on the far side of the
bay, Tom found some strange, colourful
scales. They were smaller than his
fingernails, and they stuck to the grey
rock like tiny shimmering rainbows.

As Tom picked them up, a small
green hand touched his fingers.

"What do you want with those?"
a voice asked, and a mermaid's head
appeared out of the water.

Tom got such a fright that he fell on
his bum in the wet sand.

"They're beautiful," he said. "But
you … you can have them back, of
course."

"You can keep them," the mermaid whispered. "But would you do me a favour? My pet crab has crawled into that thing over there and now he can't get out!"

With her pale green finger, she pointed at a rusty old tin the sea had washed up on the rocks. "I always tell him that I can't help him when he crawls onto dry land, but I fear that he is not a very clever little crab."

Tom nodded. "I'll have a look," he said. He tore himself away from the magical sight of the mermaid and ran to the rusty old tin. It was stuck between two rocks. Tom peeled back the lid and peeked inside.

"Careful!" the little mermaid shouted, but her warning came too late.

Tom jumped back, but the crab was already clinging to his nose with one of its claws.

"Nipper!" the mermaid shouted. "Nipper, let go this moment! How very rude!"

The crab snapped with his free claw, then let go with the other and landed in front of Tom's welly boots. He snapped his claws one more time at the strange giant in front of him and then ran as fast as his crab legs could carry him back to the mermaid.

"All right, Nipper, come here! Good crab!" the mermaid said in a voice like honey, as she let Nipper climb onto her arm.

Tom rubbed his nose. It hurt. It hurt a lot.

"I am sooooo sorry!" the mermaid said. "He is a little snappy. You should cool your nose down with sea water, or it will be twice as big by tomorrow." Tom could see that she was trying her best not to giggle.

"OK. But you keep hold of that pesky crab," he grumbled.

"I promise," the mermaid said.

Tom bent down on a rock and dipped his nose in the sea.

As Tom lifted his head from the
water, the mermaid offered him a whole
handful of shimmering scales.

"Thank you very much," she
whispered. "I am very grateful. And so
is Nipper. It's just that he just doesn't
know how to show it ..."

The crab sat on her pale green shoulder and snapped his claws. Tom still did not trust him.

But the mermaid's scales were very beautiful. He stroked them with his finger. When he lifted his head to thank her, she was gone. All that was left of her were Nipper's claw-prints in the sand.

Ben and the
Shell Surprise

Every year, Ben's parents went on
holiday to the sea. Sometimes they went
south, sometimes north, sometimes on a
ferry, sometimes on a plane – but always
to the sea.

Ben would have liked to visit a
volcano or take the lift to the 100th floor
of a skyscraper.

He had never seen the Great Wall of China, a polar bear at the North Pole, or a parrot in the rainforests of Brazil.

"Next year," his father always said. But it was next year again and here they were, back at the beach. Just like always.

"Well," Ben said to himself. "I will just have to become a deep-sea explorer." And soon he had a jar full of sand, a tin full of sea shells and all sorts of other finds. Ben's parents moaned when he put pebbles and shells in their suitcases, but they didn't take them out again.

Soon the holiday cottage was full of jars of sand, plates of sea shells and boxes of snail shells. Ben put the stones in a jar filled with water because they looked nicer when they were wet. And he kept extra-special finds in a shoe box painted to look like a treasure chest. There were crab claws in there, a piece of sea-urchin shell and a snail shell fossil.

The best thing Ben found was in a pool at the furthest end of the beach. It was hidden away by the huge rocks that lay around it, as if a giant had flung them down there. Ben peered into the water and discovered the most beautiful shells he had ever seen. There were so many of them that Ben didn't know which one to take first.

Ben took a jar out of his bag and picked one shell after the other until the jar was nearly full. Then he climbed onto the warm rocks to look at his treasure.

Ben got such a fright that he nearly dropped the jar. It was alive with creeping and crawling. Little black legs pedalled in the air, trying to grip the smooth glass as they struggled to get up the side of the jar.

At first, Ben was afraid to put his hand in, but at last he fished a shell out and had a closer look. There was a tiny crab in the shell. Its little black feet scratched Ben's fingers, as if the crab wanted to cling onto him. Ben put the shell back into the jar, fast.

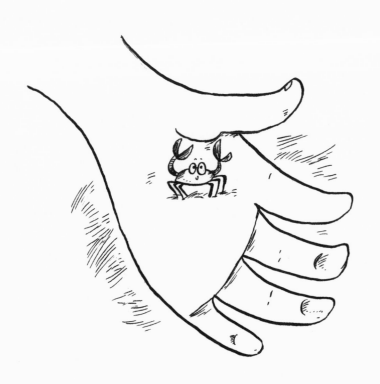

Ben looked out to sea as the crabs struggled away in the jar. After a while, he pulled out his camera and took a photo of the jar. Then he climbed back to the pool. He opened the lid of the jar with a sigh and poured the crabs back into the sea.

Ben didn't want to look at little black legs, all dead and dried up in a jar. The photo would be enough. He would only have to look at it to feel the crabs on his fingers.

All of a sudden, Ben smiled. The beach wasn't so bad, after all.

N

Rocks

Pebbly
Bay

Mermaid
Rock

Cliff Edge

Rocks

Rock
Pool

Tom's Cottage

Ella's Cottage

Anna + Max's Cottage

Ben's Cottage

Mia's Cottage

Joe + Grandpa's Cottage

SHOP

The Park

CAFE

Sandy Beach Cove